PEDRO

THE
BIG STINK

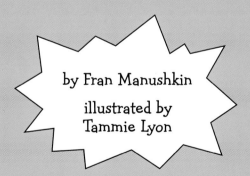

by Fran Manushkin

illustrated by
Tammie Lyon

PICTURE WINDOW BOOKS
a capstone imprint

Pedro is published by Picture Window Books,
A Capstone Imprint
1710 Roe Crest Drive
North Mankato, Minnesota 56003
www.capstonepub.com

Text © 2019 Fran Manushkin
Illustrations © 2019 Picture Window Books

Cataloging-in-Publication Data is available on the Library of Congress website.
ISBN: 978-1-5158-2820-4 (library binding)
ISBN: 978-1-5158-2825-9 (paperback)
ISBN: 978-1-5158-2836-5 (eBook PDF)

Summary: Pedro's class is learning all about the sense of smell. But when something in the room starts to stink, their lesson becomes much smellier than Miss Winkle planned for! Where is the stink coming from, and whose nose will hunt it out?

Designer: Kayla Rossow
Design Elements by Shutterstock

Printed and bound in the United States.
PA021

Table of Contents

Chapter 1

A Smelly Lesson

"Today," said Miss Winkle, "we will study our sense of smell."

"I should get my cat," said JoJo. "Her breath is smelly."

"No thanks," said Miss Winkle.

"My dad's gym socks are stinky," said Katie. "I can bring them."

"No thanks again," said Miss Winkle.

"Our noses can pick out a trillion smells," said Miss Winkle. "Let's see if you can guess some. Pablo will pass them out."

Pablo was the new boy. He was kind of quiet.

Katie Woo sniffed and said,

"This smells like a pencil."

"Smart sniffing!"

said Miss Winkle.

"But polar bears have better

noses than humans. They can

smell a seal through three feet

of ice."

"My dog can smell a burger in his sleep," bragged Pedro. He smelled his box. "I smell a potato chip," he said.

"Pew!" yelled Barry. "I got onions!"

Then it was time for lunch.

Pedro and Pablo ate together.

Pedro traded half of his

cheese sandwich for part of

Pablo's taco.

After lunch, everyone

played soccer. When Pablo got

the ball, Roddy yelled, "Beat

it, shrimp! You're too small to

play with us."

Pedro didn't say anything.

Chapter 2
Something Stinks

After lunch, Miss Winkle

told the class, "While I was

eating, I was thinking of funny

ways we talk about smells.

When we don't trust someone,

we say, 'I smell a rat.'"

"Hey," said Pedro, sniffing, "I smell something stinky right now."

"Me too," said JoJo.

"Me three," yelled Roddy.

"Maybe," said Miss Winkle. "I'm not sure."

Everyone began sniffing and searching.

"It's not coming from Binky," said Barry. "His cage is clean."

"So is our turtle's," said Katie.

"It's Pablo!" Roddy pointed.

"Our classroom never smelled

until he came."

Everyone stared at Pablo.

He looked like he might cry.

Nobody said anything.

At first, Pedro was quiet too.

But then he stood up. He

said, "Pablo does not stink. But

I know what does: It's when we

don't stick up for someone who

is being picked on."

Roddy turned red. He said,

"I was only joking."

"No you weren't," said Katie.

"And that hurt."

"I'm sorry," Roddy told Pablo.

They shook hands on it.

Chapter 3
A Stink Solved!

Suddenly Katie yelled, "I know what that smell is: It's a rotten egg."

"Ew!" said JoJo.

"Pew!" yelled everyone else.

"We have to find it!" said

Pedro. He and Pablo searched

together.

Pablo pointed. "That's

where it's coming from: Miss

Winkle's closet!"

Miss Winkle ran over

and opened the door. She

grabbed her purse and found

something in the bottom.

"Oh my!" she said. "Here's

the rotten egg!"

"I brought it for lunch yesterday but I ate a hot lunch instead. I have a cold today, so I couldn't smell it."

Miss Winkle said, "Roddy and Pablo, please toss out this rotten egg."

"Easy peasy," said Roddy.

"Easy peasy." Pablo smiled.

After school, they played soccer. Roddy told Pablo, "You are small, but quick!"

Pablo told Roddy, "You are pretty good too."

"Sometimes," said Roddy.

When Pedro got home, he told his dad, "Ask me how school was today."

"How was it?" asked his dad.

"It was smelly!" Pedro smiled, and he told him all about it.

About the Author

Fran Manushkin is the author of
many popular picture books, including
Happy in Our Skin; *Baby, Come Out!*;
*Latkes and Applesauce: A Hanukkah
Story*; *The Tushy Book*; *Big Girl
Panties*; *Big Boy Underpants*; and
Bamboo for Me, Bamboo for You!
There is a real Katie Woo—she's Fran's great-niece—
but she never gets in half the trouble of the Katie
Woo in the books. Fran writes on her beloved Mac
computer in New York City, without the help of her
two naughty cats, Chaim and Goldy.

About the Illustrator

Tammie Lyon began her love for
drawing at a young age while sitting
at the kitchen table with her dad.
She continued her love of art and
eventually attended the Columbus
College of Art and Design, where
she earned a bachelor's degree in
fine art. After a brief career as
a professional ballet dancer, she
decided to devote herself full time to illustration.
Today she lives with her husband, Lee, in
Cincinnati, Ohio. Her dogs, Gus and Dudley,
keep her company as she works in her studio.

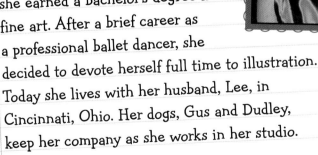

Glossary

brag (BRAG)—to talk in a boastful way about how good you are at something

breath (BRETH)—the air you take into your lungs and breathe out again

rotten (ROT-uhn)—having gone bad or started to decay due to fungi or bacteria

sense (SENSS)—one of the powers a living being uses to learn about its surroundings. Sight, hearing, touch, taste, and smell are the five senses.

shrimp (SHRIMP)—a very small or unimportant person or thing

stinky (STING-kee)—giving off a strong, unpleasant smell

trillion (TRIL-yuhn)—a very large number

Let's Talk

1. Talk about how to be a good friend. Who acted like a friend in this book? Could some characters have been better friends?

2. How do you think Pablo felt at recess? Explain your answer.

3. "I smell a rat" is an idiom. Talk about what these other smell idioms mean:
   - Stop and smell the roses.
   - Something smells fishy.
   - We came out smelling like roses.

Let's Write

1. Write down three facts about the sense of smell. If you don't know three, ask a grown-up to help you find some in a book or on the computer.

2. List five things that smell great. Then list five things that smell awful.

3. Write a story about an animal that uses the sense of smell to solve a mystery.

JOKE AROUND

✻ Why can't a nose be 12 inches long?
Because then it would be a foot.

✻ Have you heard
the joke about the
skunk?
It really stinks.

✻ What smells the
best at dinner?
your nose

✻ What did one snowman
say to the other?
"Do you smell
carrots?"

❋ What did the left eye say to
the right eye?
"Something between us
smells."

❋ What's blue and smells like
red paint?
blue paint

❋ Knock, knock
Who's there?
Nose
Nose who?
I nose plenty more knock-
knock jokes, don't worry!

THE FUN DOESN'T STOP HERE!

Discover more at www.capstonekids.com

- ✽ Videos & Contests
- ✽ Games & Puzzles
- ✽ Friends & Favorites
- ✽ Authors & Illustrators

Find cool websites and more books like this one at www.facthound.com. Just type in the Book ID: 9781515828204 and you're ready to go!